THOMAS FORD MEMORIAL LIBRARY

P9-DFT-675

3 1008

I heart you,

You haunt me

More heart-pumping reads
from Simon Pulse

Wake
Lisa McMann

Unleashed
Kristopher Reisz

Uninvited
Amanda Marrone

The Uglies series
Scott Westerfeld

Crank
and
Burned
Ellen Hopkins

I heart you,
You haunt me

Lisa Schroeder

THOMAS FORD MEMORIAL LIBRARY
800 Chestnut Street
Western Springs, IL 60558

Simon Pulse

NEW YORK   LONDON   TORONTO   SYDNEY

If you purchased this book without a cover, you should be aware that this book is stolen property. It was reported as "unsold and destroyed" to the publisher, and neither the author nor the publisher has received any payment for this "stripped book."

This book is a work of fiction. Any references to historical events, real people, or real locales are used fictitiously. Other names, characters, places, and incidents are the product of the author's imagination, and any resemblance to actual events or locales or persons, living or dead, is entirely coincidental.

SIMON PULSE
An imprint of Simon & Schuster Children's Publishing Division
1230 Avenue of the Americas, New York, NY 10020
Copyright © 2008 by Lisa Schroeder
All rights reserved, including the right of reproduction
in whole or in part in any form.
SIMON PULSE and colophon are registered trademarks
of Simon & Schuster, Inc.
Designed by Mike Rosamilia
The text of this book was set in MetaBook Roman.
Manufactured in the United States of America
First Simon Pulse edition January 2008
2 4 6 8 10 9 7 5 3
Library of Congress Control Number 2007929118
ISBN-13: 978-1-4169-5520-7
ISBN-10: 1-4169-5520-8

For Scott—

I heart you

Acknowledgments

MY HEART OVERFLOWS WITH GRATITUDE FOR SO MANY PEOPLE!

♥ Sara Crowe—thank you for your belief in this book from the beginning, and for saying different is good. You're the best!

♥ Michael del Rosario—what can I say except you are some kind of wonderful, and I so appreciate your enthusiasm.

♥ Jayme Carter, Tanya Seale, and Meg O'Hair—thank you for your willingness to read Ava and Jackson's story, and for your ideas, your suggestions, and most of all, your encouragement.

♥ Lisa—thanks for creating my music to write by. You rock!

♥ Mrs. Smith, my favorite English teacher—I'm forever grateful for all that I learned from you.

♥ Margie and Dolores—thanks for being my biggest cheerleaders!

♥ To my mom, my dad, my brother, and the Schroeders—your love and support mean the world to me.

♥ Last but definitely not least, Scott, Sam, and Grant—I thank you from the bottom of my heart for letting me do that which I love to do, and loving me every step of the way. It wouldn't mean anything if I didn't have you.

A Way of Black

I've never been
to a funeral
until today.

I see
dazzling arrangements of
red, yellow, and purple flowers
with long, green stems.

I see
a stained-glass window with
a white dove,
a yellow sun,
a blue sky.

I see
a gold cross,
standing tall,
shiny,
brilliant.

And I see
black.

Black dresses.
Black pants.
Black shoes.
Black bibles.

Black is my favorite color.
Jackson asked me about it one time.

"Ava, why don't you like pink?
Or yellow?
Or blue?"

"I love black," I said.
"It suits me."

"I suit you," he said.

And then he kissed me.

I'm not so sure
I love black
anymore.

Colorless

And then,
beyond the flowers,
beneath the stained-glass window,
beside the cross,
I see
the white casket.

I see
red, burning love
disappear
forever.

Broken Promises

My mom reaches over
and pulls my hand
from my mouth
where I chew on
the little flap of skin
along the side of my thumb
since I have no more nails
left to chew on.

An ugly habit.
One I promised Jackson
I would break.

I wonder,
do you have to keep a promise
to a dead person?

Mom holds my hand
in hers as the
music starts to play.

Jackson's
smiling face
appears on the screen
as we hear Eric Clapton's
haunting song
Tears in Heaven.

It's not long
before tears in heaven
make their way

to my eyes,
so I close them
for a second.

From out of nowhere,
I'm in his car, by his side.
Music playing.
Windows rolled down.
I kick off my shoes,
put my bare feet on the dashboard
and put my hand in his.

"Never leave me, okay?" I say to him.

"Okay," he tells me.

He squeezes my hand,
like that seals the deal.

My gaze
returns to the
beautiful boy
on the screen
while
my thumb
returns
to my mouth.

He broke his promise.
I can break mine.

I Will Always Remember

The minister speaks.

"It is hard when a young life is tragically cut short.

"But we must celebrate the life that was Jackson's.

"Look around at the friends and the family
who loved Jackson Montgomery.

"You will keep the memory of him alive."

There is *one* memory
that floods my brain
every five minutes.

It reminds me
over
and over
and over again,
I'm the reason
my boyfriend
is gone.

Memories might keep him alive.

But they might
kill
me.

No Words

After the service,
people get in line
to tell the family,
"I'm sorry,"
"He was so young,"
and
"Let me know if I can do anything."

I'm one of the
first people
in line
because
I want to get it over with.

His mom is there
and I try to say
"I'm sorry"
like I'm supposed to,
but the words
won't come
from my brain
to my mouth
like they're supposed to.

She looks at me
and I feel her eyes
piercing my heart,
making it hurt
even more.

She probably blames me
like I blame myself.
I can't blame her
for that.

She tries to smile.
She asks politely,
with no feeling,
because she has to say
something,

"Are you okay, Ava?"

I nod,
but inside
my heart is screaming
and kicking
and stomping,
throwing a tantrum
like a two-year-old
because
I am definitely
not okay.

She hugs me.
A quick hug.
A fake hug.
An I'm-only-hugging-you-because-I-don't-know-what-else-to-do hug.

Next,
I hug
the people
Jackson loved
most
in the whole,
wide
world.

His sister,
then his brother.

I tell myself
to be strong.

I should be strong
for them.

But I'm not.

I sob
into Daniel's
black jacket.

"Shhhhhhhhh," he whispers.
"You're going to get through this."

Just like his brother,
thinking about me,
not himself.

After that,
I stand alone
and wait for my mom
so we can
leave.

There is no line of people coming up to me
to say "I'm sorry"
or "He was so young"
or "Let me know if I can do anything."

It feels like everyone
is looking at me.
What are they thinking?
Do I even want to know?

And then,
like an unexpected rain shower
on a day that's so dry
you can't breathe,
there is Cali
squeezing me tight
and Jessa
holding my hand
and Zoe
rubbing my back.

In that moment,
I realize
a circle of love
is ten times better
than a procession
of sorrys.

The Boy

Another procession.

This time,
a line of cars
driving
to the cemetery.

Mom calls Dad
on her cell.

He's on a business trip in Paris.
He offered to come home.
I told him it'd be okay.
I have Mom, and besides,
what could he do?

I hear Mom say,

"Beautiful service . . ."

"She's hanging in there. . . ."

"Wish you could be here. . . ."

"Wanna talk to Ava?"

I shake my head
and wave my hand
to tell her no.

There's nothing to say
that she hasn't said already.

"I guess she's tired right now. . . ."

I make myself
drift back
to a happier time.

Jackson came to our school
in the fall
from a different school
in a different town.

He was the boy
with the shaved head
and the little goatee.

He looked old
for a junior.

The four of us,
Cali, Jessa, Zoe, and me,
talked about him
at lunch,
eating tacos,
Cali's favorite food.

"Maybe he had cancer," Jessa said,
"and lost his hair."

"That's terrible," Cali said.

"Maybe he thinks bald is sexy," Zoe said.

"On him," I said, "it is."

He Spiced Up My Life

When you meet someone
so different from yourself,
in a *good* way,
you don't even have to kiss
to have fireworks go off.

It's like fireworks
in your heart
all the time.

I always wondered,
do opposites really attract?
Now I know for sure
they do.

I'd grown up
going to the library as often
as most people go
to the grocery store.

Jackson didn't need to read
about exciting people and places.
He went out
and found them,
or created excitement himself
if there wasn't any
to be found.

The things I like are
pretty simple.

Burning CDs around themes,
like Songs to Get Your Groove On and
Tunes to Fix a Broken Heart;
watching movies;
baking cookies;
and swimming.

It's like I was a garden salad with a light vinaigrette,
and Jackson was a platter of seafood Cajun pasta.

Alone, we were good.
Together, we were fantastic.

The Final Good-bye

Ashes

    to

        ashes.

Dust

    to

        dust.

I think
this is where
I'm supposed to say
good-bye.

Is that what
everyone's thinking?
Good-bye, Jackson?
Rest in peace?

That's not what I'm thinking.

I'm thinking,
I hate good-byes.

"Let us pray," the minister says.

Dear God,
> *What can I do?*
> *He didn't deserve this.*
> *Can't we bring him back?*
> *Isn't there anything that will bring him back?*
> *Please?*
> *Amen*

I look around.

If tears
could bring him back,
there'd be enough
to bring him back
a hundred times.

It's Not Fair

Mom takes my hand
and leads me back
to the car.

All I can think about
is how my boyfriend
will soon be
underground.

He'll be lying there
alone
in the dirt.

Mom asks me
if I want to go to the Montgomery house,
where people will gather
to eat
and talk
and remember.

"I can't believe people feel like eating.
And talking.
Those are the last things I want to do."

"Life goes on, honey," Mom says.

As we pull away,
my eyes stay glued
to the casket.

It's proof
that sometimes
life
does
not
go
on.

As Two Names No More

Ava + Jackson = true LOVE 4ever

I ♥ Jackson

J loves A
A loves J

Scribbles I made
on my French notebook.

I study the words
on the purple notebook
like I used to study
Jackson's face
when he wasn't looking.

When we got home,
Mom suggested
I write down my feelings.
Basically, keep a journal.

But I can't stop staring
at those scribbles
and thinking about how
they used to be true.
But not anymore.

Now it's just Ava.

No more Jackson.
No more true LOVE 4ever.

I turn the
tear-splattered cover.
I put the pen to the page.
All I can write is
Jackson
Jackson
Jackson

Jumps In

I started swimming
about the time
I traded my bottle
for a sippy cup.

Mom took me to
a Baby and Me class
at the pool.

She said I was so natural
in the water,
she wondered
if she'd actually given birth
to a mermaid.

By high school
I was swimming competitively
on the swim team.

Jackson came
and watched me swim
many times.

That's where it started.

"I dare you to jump off the high dive," he said
one day after practice.

"You know I'm afraid of heights!"

"Exactly. That's why I'm daring you."

I couldn't
disappoint
my boyfriend.
I climbed the ladder,
making sure I didn't look down.

I inched my way
to the edge of the board,
then I crossed my fingers,
closed my eyes,
said a prayer,
and

       jumped.

My stomach flew
to my throat
as the air
rushed
around me
and through me
until
I hit that water hard.

"I did it!" I yelled
as I climbed out of the pool.

He brought me a towel and simply said,
"That's my girl."

Nothing to Do Now

This summer,
I could have made money
at my second home.

I could have sat by the pool
in my suit,
pretending to watch the kids,
to guard lives,
while I thought about
him.

But accidents happen that way.
And my life doesn't need any more
accidents.

So today I quit my job.

Mom asks me, "What are you going to do all summer?"

I just shrug.

Lashing Out

Nick,
my ex-boyfriend,
my boyfriend
pre-Jackson,
calls me.

"Ava?"

"Yeah."

"I've been thinking about you.
Are you okay?"

"Nick, that's a freaking ridiculous question."

"Is there anything I can do?"

"Nope. Not a thing.
Good-bye, Nick."

Click.

Crap, why did I *do* that?
He was just trying to be nice.

I'm such a jerk.

Is being a jerk
one of the five
stages of grief?

Wishful Thinking

I'm sitting
on the porch swing,
thinking of how
Jackson and I
used to
sit and swing
together.

The stars are duller
than an old pocketknife.
They used to sparkle
like five-carat diamonds.

I wonder,
is heaven
up in the stars?
Beyond the stars?

Can Jackson see them
like I see them?

Is he wishing
like I'm wishing?

"Star light, star bright," he said the first time
we sat here together.

"Make my wish come true tonight," I said.

"That's not how it goes."

"Why drag it out?" I asked.

He laughed. "So, what's your wish?"

"That time would stop,
so we could stay like this forever."

"Tough wish," he said.

"What about you?" I asked.

"Let's see.
I'm hungry.
How about a cheeseburger?"

"How romantic," I told him.

"Change your wish to a chocolate shake and we're set."

We went to In-N-Out Burger after that.

He got his wish.

I didn't get mine.

I Need Mr. Sandman

Sleep doesn't come.
Night after night
I thrash around
like a fish
caught in a net
trying to escape.

And I cry
for what I've done
and who I've lost.

Four days after the funeral,
Mom shows me the phone messages
she's taken for me.

I didn't want to talk
to anyone.

Jackson's brother, Daniel, called.
Jessa and Zoe called.
Nick called,
again.

I ball them up
and throw them away.

"You're tired," Mom says.

She calls the doctor.
He prescribes Ambien.

"That's good," Mom says.
"Sleep will help."

Will anything *really* help?

When I wake up,
I remember.

It hurts
to remember.

Mom brings me a sandwich
and some juice.
I get up to pee
and sneak another pill.

"I need to sleep a little more," I tell Mom.

She doesn't argue.

Because sleep helps.

Company's Coming

The phone rings.
It rings and rings.
I finally drag
my butt out of bed
and answer it.

"Ava?"

"Yeah."

"Do you want to do something?" Cali asks.
"Maybe go to the pool?"

"Not really."

"Wanna do something else?"

"Not really."

"Are you okay?"

"Not really."

"Can I come over?"

"I guess."

"You need anything?"

But before I can answer, she says, "Never mind.
Stupid question."

Stupid.
But sweet.

Mirror, Mirror

I'm putting on makeup.
I'll be like a clown
and no one will see
the real face
behind the mask.

I don't want Cali to see
the sad me,
the depressed me,
the shamed me.

As I stand in the bathroom,
carefully lining my eyelids
bronze,
I feel a splash
of cool air.

I shiver.

I feel something.
Something behind me.
Something familiar.
Hauntingly familiar.

I glance behind me,
but I don't see
anything.
Or anyone.

And then,
when I look in the mirror
again,
I see,
for a split second,
not just me,
but someone else.

Jackson.

Food for Thought

Cali's knocking,
so I turn and run.

As I run down the stairs,
I'm thinking there must be such a thing
as too much sleep.

That wasn't really him.
It couldn't have been him.

Could it?

When I open the door,
she gives me her
best girlfriend hug
and I realize
how much I have missed
my Cali.

We go to the kitchen,
plop down at the table.

"Thanks for coming," I say.

She looks at her watch.
"You hungry?"

"I could eat."

I get up
and open the pantry door.

I don't even know
if it's time for breakfast
or lunch
or dinner.

"What time is it?" I ask.

"11:00."

I stand there, staring at the boxes
of crackers
and cereal,
trying to focus
on food
and not
on what I just saw
in the mirror.

The cool air
surrounds me again.
I get goose bumps.
I feel him, standing there,
next to me,
like he's hungry too,
looking for something to eat.

"Did you feel that?" I ask.

"What?" she says.

"Nothing."

She'll think I'm crazy.
Maybe she'd be right.

And then,
there's the slightest hint of
something brushing
my cheek.

Not a touch,
less than a touch.
A whisper.
No, a feeling.
Just a feeling.
Or maybe,
just my imagination.

I shiver again.

Am I going crazy?

"I think you need to get out," Cali says.
"Let's go to the mall.
For some yummy food court food,
and a little shopping, if you want."

I shrug. "I guess."

This is good.
I'm a normal girl
going to the mall.
Not crazy.

Not a girl
who's beginning to think
she's being haunted
by her
dead
boyfriend.

Okay or Not Okay?

Cali has a green VW bug.
Cute.
Fun.
Perfect.
Like Cali.

I was going to work
so I could buy a car
when I turn sixteen
on August 15th.

Oh well.

All the things that
used to be so important
aren't important
anymore.

"We haven't been to the mall together in a long time," Cali says.

"Yeah.
The last time I was there, Jackson bought me—"

I stop.
I look out the window.
There's an old man
with an old woman,
sitting on a bench,
waiting for the bus.

He's looking at a newspaper.
She's looking at him.
She says something.
He looks at her.
He smiles.
She smiles.

The scene is so simple,
so lovely,
so perfect.

"It's okay to talk about him," Cali says.

"I know."

"What did he buy you?"

I don't want to say.
But she asked.

"That black-and-pink bikini.
To wear to the School's Out party."

She nods.
She remembers.
If she had known
it would bring up
that tragic day,
she wouldn't have asked.

She shakes her head.
Turns the radio up.

I guess sometimes
it's not okay
to talk about
him.

Cali

As she fiddles with the radio,
Cali's blue-and-purple bracelet
twists and slides
on her arm.

The summer
between fifth and sixth grades,
we rode our bikes
to the pool
almost every day.

Then we came home
and made necklaces and bracelets
out of beads.

We loved
sitting
and talking
and making
beautiful jewelry
together.

We sold our creations
to kids in the neighborhood.
My dad called us *little entrepreneurs*.
I called us *best friends*.

"You still wear the bracelet I made for you," I say,
thinking how it's so amazing
she's kept it
all this time.

"I love it.
Where's the one I made for you?"

"I lost it."

"I'll make you another one," she says.
"We can buy some beads at the mall."

That's Cali.
The one who will do
anything for me.

Thank God for Cali.

Wondering

I shop,
but I don't buy.

I eat,
but I don't taste.

Cali talks,
but I don't listen.

My mind's drifting,
thinking about him.

Wondering if I'll feel that cool air,
feel that brush against my cheek,
feel Jackson again,
when I go home.

It couldn't have been him.
I'm being ridiculous.

Still,
it's not long before
I want to go home
and find out
for sure.

The Way My Life Changed

I lean my head back
on the car seat
as we drive home.

With my eyes closed,
I search for a memory
that will make me
smile.

And then,
I remember the night
my life changed
forever.

The silver bleachers
filled with kids
in black and red,
cheering the football team
to victory.

It was a warm September night.
The best kind of Friday night.
My favorite kind of high school night.

He was two rows up.
Behind me.
Watching me.
Or so he told me later.

Cali, Jessa, and Zoe
went to get us food.

I stayed
to save our seats.
And that's when
he made his move.

"Hi."

"Hi."

"I'm Jackson."

"I know.
Everyone knows who you are."

His cheeks turned
the color of watermelon.
His eyes greener
than the rind.

He was *so* cute,
from the top of his sexy bald head
to the tips of his PacSun shoes.

The way he looked at me
made me quiver
and quake.

It was a good thing
I was sitting down.
My legs wouldn't have
held me up.

Who Are You?

"Do you know who I am?" I asked.

"No. But I'd like to."

"Ava Bender."

"Ava,"
he said.
"I like that name.
Ava."

I *loved* the way
he said my name.

He talked about the game,
and about his old school.
He talked about how moving sucked,
and about being the new kid,
which sucked even more.

I talked about living in the same house
my whole life
with a mom who works a lot
and a dad who travels a lot.

"Tell me something about Ava no one else knows," he said.

"No one?"

I had to think hard
on that one.

"I really hate being alone," I finally said.

"Then it's a good thing I'm here."

That made me smile.

"Now it's your turn," I told him.

"I want to go out with you."

That made me smile
even more.

I couldn't say anything
because my friends came back.

Jackson didn't move.
They squeezed in
on the other side of me.
I introduced them.

They looked at me
like I'd just won
the lottery.

But it was *way* better
than that.

The Other Side

The green bug
backs away.

I wave
and smile
like everything's fine,
while inside
I'm freaking out
because I don't know
if he's waiting for me
on the other side
of that door.

Awake

I move from one room
to the next.
Downstairs.
Upstairs.
I whisper his name.
"Jackson?
How do I find you?"

I go to the bathroom
and stare into the mirror.

I look more awake
than I've been
in weeks.

Like a kid
who wakes up *really* early
on Christmas day
and can't wait
to see what's under
the tree.

I stand in front of the mirror
for minutes.
Maybe hours.

"Ava, I'm home," Mom calls from downstairs.
"Are you awake?"

Suddenly,
the air temperature drops,
and this time
there's no confusion.

Jackson's face
flashes
next to mine.

I'd say
awake
is an
understatement.

Home Is Where the Heart Is

Mom makes spaghetti.
She makes it
because I love it.
And because she's happy
I'm awake.

"Feeling better?" she asks.

"Yeah.
Cali took me to the mall."

"Good.
I was starting to worry."

"Mom, it's Thursday, right?"

"Yes."

"Dad comes home tomorrow?"

"Yes," she says. "Should we go to the beach this weekend?"

No.
NO!
I don't want to go anywhere.
If Jackson's here,
I have to stay here.

"Can we just stay home?
Watch some movies?"

She smiles.
"That sounds nice."

"Thanks for the spaghetti.
It was good."

"You're welcome, sweetheart."

It's Nick Again

Nick calls Thursday night,
to express
his concern for me
one more time.

I tell him I'm okay,
and there's nothing he can do
because I just buried my boyfriend
and of course I'm really not
that
okay.

"I just want you to know I'm here for you, Ava.
If you need me."

It's weird.
Does he want a second chance?
Does he want to be the rebound guy?

Or maybe
he is loving
every minute
of my grief
and unhappiness.

Maybe he's thinking
I had it coming.

And maybe,
just maybe,
I did.

What Did It Mean?

Dare:
a challenge
to do something dangerous
or foolhardy.

I dare you.

Three
stupid
words.

I dared him to order octopus at a restaurant and to eat it *all*.
He dared me to write a love letter, sign it Secret Admirer, and
sneak it to a teacher.
I dared him to pretend he was blind in the crystal section of
the department store.

This game,
or whatever it was,
became our little
thing.

Jackson,
the rock climber,
the white-water rafter,
the extreme skier guy,
loved the feel of adrenaline
ROARING
through his veins.

For me,
it was scary,
and exhilarating,
all at the same time.
But I could have lived
without it.

All I needed
was Jackson.

I wish all he'd needed
was me.

A Strange Sensation

I can hear my heart
beat
beat
beating
in the darkness
as I try
to go to sleep.

The clock says 12:08.

Mom is asleep by now.

I get up
and go down the stairs
to make hot cocoa.

Will he be there,
waiting for me?

My heart is
beat
beat
beating
faster,
even though
there's no sign of him.

When the hot cocoa is done,
I put marshmallows in.
I stir slowly,
watching them melt
into each other.

I think of Jackson.
His touch,
his kisses,
and the way he looked at me,
with eyes like a green ocean.

I take a sip,
and the cocoa's so hot
it burns my tongue.

Hot.
Cold.
Hot.
Cold.

I shiver.

"Jackson?"

Smells Like Sandalwood

I spin
around
and around
and around
like a top on a wooden floor.

"Where are you?
Show me you're here.
Please?"

I stop.
I stand still.
I wait.

There is just enough light
from the full moon
shining through the
kitchen window.

The white, frilly curtains
move slightly.
Shifting.
Fluttering.

And then I smell
the smell that was all
Jackson,
because he kept that head
and beautiful face
so well shaven.

Sandalwood
shaving
cream.

Music Says It All

I sit down
at the kitchen table
and I whisper,
like he is sitting
right across from me.

"Jackson, I know it's you.
I'm not scared.
Maybe I should be, but I'm not.
Whatever you need to do to talk to me,
in your own way, is okay.
I'm not scared.

"Can I see you?
I want to see you."

Nothing happens.

I ask him, "Don't ghosts or spirits or whatever
sometimes show themselves?"

And then
the CD player
on the kitchen counter
starts to play.

3 Doors Down.
Here By Me.

Skinless

The music's loud.
It makes me

jump

right out of my skin.

I run over
and turn it down.

As I do,
I see the slightest reflection
of Jackson
on the stainless steel fridge.

"Oh, God.
It's really you.
Jackson.
You're here."

I feel him
move closer to me.
The smell of him
fills me up.
It makes the hairs
on my arms
stand up straight.

"Can I touch you?" I whisper.

No answer.

I guess,
in order to
touch,
there has to be skin,
which a ghost
doesn't have.

I Can Hear You

There's
a murmur
inside my brain,
so quiet,
I have to close my eyes tight
and really concentrate
to hear it.

Ava,
I'm here.
I can't talk this way often.
It's hard to get my thoughts
through to you.
Just know
I love you,
and I'm not going to leave you.

Dancing in the Moonlight

I whisper back.

"I understand.
You don't have to talk.
You don't have to do anything.
Just you being here
is enough.
I'm *so* glad you're here, Jackson."

I have more I want to say.
But not now.
Now is the time
to just be together.

"Dance with me," I whisper.

I get up, and sway to the music.
My eyes are closed.
I imagine him there,
with me in the moonlight,
hugging me,
caressing me,
loving me.

And I know
with all of my
Jackson-loving heart
that's exactly
what he's doing.

But then
the music turns off
and the room
warms up.

He's gone.

Trust Me

A few seconds later,
Mom appears.
She flicks on the light
and I squint my eyes
at the brightness.

"Ava?
Are you okay?
I thought I heard music.
Were you playing music?"

"Sorry, Mom.
I came down to have cocoa.
I turned the CD player on.
Sorry it woke you up."

She reaches out
and hugs me.

"Why are you shaking?" she asks.
"Did I scare you?"

There's no way I can tell her.

"I guess a little.
But I'm okay.
Ready for bed."

She keeps her arm
around me
and we go upstairs
together.

"You sure you're okay?" she asks
when we get to my room.

I smile.

"Better than ever."

The Next Morning

What if it was
just
a
dream?

Lovely Lemons

I wait all day,
wandering the house,
but there is no sign
of him.

If he said he isn't going to leave me,
why does it seem like
he's left me?

Maybe being a ghost is
more complicated
than I understand.

I make fresh lemonade,
squeezing the lemons
Mom brought home
yesterday.

Lemons are one of
my favorite things.

Luscious
and juicy,
they remind me
of Jackson's
kisses.

I remember the time
we went out for dessert.

He had chocolate cake.
I had a lemon tart.

"You have lemon," Jackson said,
"in the corner of your mouth.
Let me get it for you."

And just like that
he leaned in
and kissed me,
his tongue
gently licking
the lemon
away.

That's how it was with us.
Comfortable.
Easy.
So. Incredibly. Wonderful.

I add sugar,
water,
and ice cubes
to the juice
in the pitcher.

When I take a drink,
it tastes
sweet and sour
like it should be.

My heart feels
sweet and sour too.

Is that how it should be?

And then,
when the coolness
sweeps over me,
giving me goose bumps,
and I know he has returned,
everything is oh, so
sweet.

A Gift

Dad comes home.

"Angel," he says, hugging me.

He breaks away
to tell me
what I already knew.

"I'm sorry.
What a rotten time for me to be gone."

I know he's been worried about me.
He's called almost every day.

"I'm okay, Dad."

"Promise?"

"Promise."

He reaches down,
unzips his suitcase,
and pulls out a bag.

"I brought you some perfume.
They say Paris makes the best, you know."

I take it out of the bag.
A shiny, gold sun
caps the bottle.

I unscrew the sun
and take a whiff.

"I figured you could use a little sunshine about now," he tells me.

I hug him again.
"Thanks, Dad.
I'm glad you're home."

Life with a Ghost

Jackson seems
to be afraid
to come around
if my parents
are with me.

I guess if they knew
about him,
it *would* be really strange.

Dad sticks
close to me.
We talk a lot
and share ice cream
after dinner.

Finally,
I retreat
to my room.

There's a note
on my mirror
written
in toffee lipstick.

Ava
is
beautiful.

Ava
is
good.

Ava
is
mine.

I put the lipstick
on my lips
and give the mirror
a big, fat
kiss.

Not a Pity Party

Saturday morning,
Zoe calls.

"I'm having a pool party tonight," she says.
"Will you come?"

"I don't know."

"Ava, I miss you.
Please come."

I tell her I'll call her back.
I need to think about it.

"Who was that?" Mom asks.

"Zoe.
She's having a pool party tonight."

"Sounds like fun. You should go."

"But—"

I don't finish my sentence.
I can't say,
But I'd rather stay home and hang out with Jackson.

Because he's here,
and maybe we'll make hot cocoa together
or something.

Hard to Say Yes

"But what, honey?" Mom asks.
She's pouring herself
a glass of lemonade.

"Can I have some of that?" I ask.

I watch the yellow liquid
splash into the glass,
so free and sure of itself.

Zoe calls again.

"You have to come.
Nick's brother's band is going to play.
It'll be so great.
S'il vous plaît?"

Mom *begs* me with her eyes.
Zoe *begs* me with her words.

"Okay."

Zoe

Cali and I
met Zoe and Jessa
in French class,
freshman year.

We were
grouped together,
and our assignment
was to make
a French dessert
to share with the class.

We went to Zoe's house
because her dad
is a chef
and he wanted to help us.

Except we were
so giggly
and so here
and there
and everywhere
in the kitchen,
he left us alone
to make our
soufflé au chocolat.

The first one
was a flop
because we burnt
the chocolate.

But Zoe said,
"Like Napoleon,
we will not give up!"

The second time,
we were focused
and worked together,
like soldiers in an army,
battling the double boiler
with all our might.

Our *soufflé au chocolat*
turned out
magnifique.

I love a lot of things
about Zoe,
but I especially love
how she doesn't give up.

Zoe is
très magnifique.

Am I Suited for This?

I pull out the bikini.
The one Jackson bought me.
The one I wore *that* day.

I can't wear it.
I won't wear it.
Never
ever
again.

I should throw it away.
But Jackson gave it to me.
It's the last thing he gave me.
So I'll keep it.
But I won't wear it.

I pull out last year's suit
that's faded
from the sun
and the chlorine
and not *nearly* as cute
as the black-and-pink one
from Jackson.

Who cares.
It's not like I'm trying
to look hot
for a guy
or anything.

I'm just going because—

Wait a minute.
Why am I going?

Beauty Everywhere

I sit in the corner
watching
the swimmers
the dancers
the smoochers
the gabbers
the drinkers
the smokers.

"Come in, Ava," Cali yells from the pool.
"We need you!" Zoe cries.

I raise my drink in the air.
But I don't move.
I stay right
where I feel
I belong.

The sun starts to set
and tangerine orange
turns to
cotton candy pink
and I wish
my man
Jackson was here
to give me some
cranberry red love.

"Ava," I hear
in a deep voice
I recognize.

It's Nick.

Imagine that.
The boy
who won't leave me
alone.

"Hey," I say.

"You look lonely over here by yourself."

I point
to the orange-and-pink sky.

"Isn't that the most gorgeous thing you've ever seen?"

He doesn't take his eyes off me.

"Yeah. It is."

You Can't Go Back

"So what's the deal, Nick?
You stalking me?"

He laughs. "No. Just worried about you.
That's all."

"Well, please don't worry about me.
I'm fine."

I think of Jackson
at home,
where I might see him
again tonight.
I smile.

Wait.
Does Jackson follow me?
Does he know what's happening here?
Will he be pissed I'm talking to Nick?
No.
I'd feel him if he were here.
Wouldn't I?

"It's good to see you," Nick says.
"I've missed you.
I look back and wonder
how I could have been so crazy
to let you go."

"Let me go?
You cheated on me, Nick.

I cut you loose."

"So if I got up the nerve to ask you out again,
and promised to be good,
would you even consider saying yes?"

I stand up
and hand him the empty glass.

"Not in a million sunsets, Nick."

Cold Shoulder

When I get home,
it's late.

And the house is
freaking
freezing.

It feels like
I live
in an igloo.

I grab a blanket from the closet
and wrap it around my shoulders.
I head to the kitchen.

Every
single
cupboard
door
is open.

"Jackson," I whisper.
"I'm home."

The CD player turns on.

My stomach does
a somersault.

I listen,
trying to
place it.

Got it.

Don't Leave Me
by Green Day.

Freaky Saturday

"Are you mad at me for going?"

No response.
Although I don't know
what kind of response
I expected
exactly.

"Jackson, I can't stay home all the time.

"Besides, Mom and Dad would get suspicious
if I never went anywhere.

"I don't want them to know about you and me.

"They'd think I'm crazy."

All the cupboard doors
slam shut
at the
exact
same time.

Now my stomach
does a
backhand flip.

Messing with Me

"I'm going to bed,
Jackson.
I'm tired.
Good night."

I walk up the stairs.
I feel him
following me.

I tremble
as I feel cold air,
or is it breath,
on the back
of my neck.

I open the door to my room
and gasp.

My panties
and bras
and socks
and nighties
have been flung
all over
my room.

That's My Boy

I stand there for a minute
and then
I close the door
and smile.

My smile turns into
giggles.

I belly flop
onto my bed,
splashing panties
everywhere.

This is *so* Jackson.

He gets mad.
He throws a little tantrum.
We laugh about it.

I remember
the time
I decided to go
to the day spa
with my girlfriends
instead of hanging
with him.

He waited outside the spa
until we walked up.

He pulled me aside,
all pissed off,
and told me
I *totally* ruined his day.

He said, "I had something special planned."

"Special?" I asked,
wondering what exactly *that* meant.

He shrugged
and pulled two
basketball tickets
out of his pocket.

I burst out laughing and
punched him in the arm.
"Basketball is *not* special!"

He couldn't help it.
He started laughing too.

Then he pulled me
into his arms
and whispered
in my ear,
"I just love you so much.
I want to be with you always."

It's like I can hear him
repeating those words now.

I go to work
putting all the stuff back
where it belongs.

The room starts to warm up,
which makes
the ice in the igloo
start to
m
  e
    l
    t
and I whisper into
the silence of the night,
"I want to be with you always too."

Like a warm summer breeze
in my head,
I hear his words.
This is so hard for me, Ava.
I want it to be like it was before.
I'll try to be more understanding.
Please forgive me?

Like he even
has to ask.

The Sea of Love

When exhaustion
finally hits me,
I fall into bed.

It's not long
before I'm in that
strange place
between asleep
and awake,
where you might
fall off a cliff
or find a stranger
chasing you.

But tonight,
waiting for me
behind the magical
curtain of dreams,
there's Jackson,
as clear as the
sparkling silver tips
of the sea
that surround the boat
we're rocking in.

We face each other,
the full moon
so iridescent,
it reminds me of

the glow-in-the-dark planets
I used to have
on my ceiling.

We stand there
in peaceful darkness,
not talking,
not touching,
but feeling
volts of electricity
charging through our veins.

When he finally
reaches out
to touch me,
the energy
is so intense,
I jump.

He pulls me to him
and kisses me,
his lips
so soft,
so delicious,
so *real*,
I can't help
but reach up
and touch them
with my fingers.

And once I feel his skin
beneath my fingers,
I want more.

It's like he's a map
and I'm trying to find
my way home.

While we kiss,
my hands travel
across his chest,
down his arms,
to his hands,
where our
fingers
intertwine.

We raise
our hands
in the air
above us,
victorious in love,
only to let go
and push ourselves
together
even closer.

When we
release our lips,
we both

g   a   s   p
for air.

Then,
he cradles my body
as he ever-so-gently
lays my
q
u
i
v
e
r
i
n
g
body
down.

Our eyes locked,
my finger
traces his jaw.
Before I can say
I love you,
I'm swimming
in the
warm sea
of his
kisses
once again.

Question of the Day

Can a girl
lose her
virginity
to a
ghost?

Christmas in Paris

It's Sunday morning
and Dad takes me out
for breakfast.

I get pancakes with strawberries
and whipped cream.

Dad orders pigs in a blanket.

We both have coffee
with sugar.
Lots and lots of sugar.

Dad talks about Paris
and how he'd love to take me
and Mom there
someday.

He says I'd love the Eiffel Tower,
the Arc de Triomphe,
the Louvre,
the cafés,
the shopping.

"Let's go at Christmastime," he says.

I think of my three best friends.
They would *love* to go to Paris.

Why not me?

3 1308 00257 5017

Maybe it's because
Paris is *really*
far away
and we would have to
stay away from home
for a *really*
long time.

You Lift Me Up

On the way home
Dad drives past the place
where the city's festival
is held every spring.

Jackson took me
to the carnival.
We rock-and-rolled
on the roller coaster
and French-kissed
on the merry-go-round
and laughed hysterically
on the hammerhead.

We ate corn dogs
and curly fries
and raspberry scones.

"I want one of those!" I said,
pointing to the big stuffed teddy bears
hanging above the
MILK CAN SOFTBALL TOSS.

Jackson stuck his chest out
and said, "No problem!"

Twenty dollars later
I was stuck with
a teeny-tiny
yellow
stuffed
snake.

"How appropriate," Jackson told me.
"These guys are so slimy.
'Step right up!
We'll take all your money,
and even better,
make you look like a loser
in front of your girlfriend!'"

I laughed
and told him
I loved my
teeny-tiny snake
and who needs
a big, old teddy bear
anyway,
when I have a perfectly
good boyfriend
to cuddle with.

With his last dollar,
he turned to the man
selling balloons
and bought me
a red one.

"A balloon *and* a snake?
This is my lucky day!"

But as he reached out
to hand me the balloon,
I didn't quite have a grip
on the string.

As we watched   and away,
the balloon   up
float   up
                  up

Jackson whispered into my ear,
"Ava,
you are my helium."

He was always good
at making the best of things.

Daddy's Little Girl

The tears roll down my face,
without notice,
without effort,
but with feeling.

I thought I was done crying.
I mean, Jackson's come back to me.

And yet, there won't be
any more days
like that day
at the carnival.

Jackson may be back,
but those days
are gone
forever.

Dad looks over at me.
And then he turns away.
He doesn't say
anything.

What's he thinking?
That this is all for the best,
because when you're fifteen,
you shouldn't be so serious,
like he and Mom told me a few months ago?

Mom and Dad liked Jackson.
I know they did.
He stayed for dinner sometimes
and he made them laugh,
telling stories about his brother and sister
and the pranks they played on one another.

But my parents worried.
"You're so young . . ."
"You're spending too much time together. . . ."
"How serious is it . . ."

I look at Dad.
He looks at me
again.

Then his hand reaches up
and wipes the tears away,
without notice,
without effort,
but with feeling.

"I remember when you were little," he says,
"you'd fall down and scrape your knee.
And you'd come running over to me, crying and crying."

"Then you'd kiss it," I tell him,
"and make it better."

I remember too.
It was *so* easy then.

"I know you loved him a lot.
And I wish I could make this better."

So *that's*
what he was
thinking.

"I love you, Dad."

I Do What I Have to Do

The real estate business
slows down in the summer.

Mom is home
more and more.

Jackson's there
less and less.

So I endure the long days
to enjoy the sweet
but silent
nights
where he often visits
in my dreams.

I tried to talk once,
to tell him
how sorry I feel.

But he covered my lips
with his
and that was that.

At least in my dreams
I have his soothing touch.

Even in the silence,
my heart overflows
with the love
that is all
Jackson's.

I wake later
and later
and later
each day.

I search the cupboards
and drawers
for the pills
Mom gave me
so I might
sleep all the time
like I did before.

But I can't find them.

Won't Be Blue

"Come with me," Mom says.
"To the library.
Books and summertime
go together."

"No.
I don't feel well."

"Are you okay?" Mom asks.
"You've been sleeping a lot.
Maybe we should take you to the doctor."

"I'm fine, Mom.
Just have a cold or something."

So, she leaves without me.

The CD player turns on
You're The One, by Sugarcult.

A blue bouncy ball
rolls across the floor.

I pick it up.
There's scribbled writing,
hard to read.

I figure out it says:
Don't be blue.
I love you!

Let the Sunshine In

The doorbell rings.
Surprise!

I'm in my ratty robe
with pictures of sunglasses
splattered on the fabric.

I peek out and see
Cali, Zoe, and Jessa.

When I open the door,
Jessa says,
"Dude, you look like shit."

That's Jessa.
Always telling it like it is.

They don't wait for me
to invite them in.

They each give me a hug,
then plop themselves
on the couch.

"So.
What's new?" I ask.

"I got a puppy," Cali says.
"A cockapoo. I named him Gumball."

"Gumball?" I ask.

"He's *so* cute," Zoe says.

"But even bigger news is Cali met someone," Jessa blurts out.

"You did?" I ask.

"He was a senior last year," Cali says.
"But it's still early in the game.
I have to work on him some more.
Get him to ask me out."

As she talks,
I notice how gorgeous
they all look
in their tank tops
and shorts,
their tan legs
and painted toes.

They look
how California girls
should look
in the summer.

I glance down
at myself.

I've got sunglasses
on my robe.

And that's about it
for me.

Jessa

I've always been the quiet girl.
I'm the good girl
who does
what she's told
(most of the time).

Jessa is the loud girl.
She's the bad girl
who makes you
want to be bad too,
because it looks
so good
on her,
with her pierced nose
and her wild hair.

She's the youngest
in a family
with six kids.

I think she had to be loud
and bad
so she wouldn't
be forgotten.

Jessa loves the movies.
We went to the movies together a lot,
while Cali and Zoe
played volleyball.

The first time we went,
Jessa said,
"Let's stay and see another one."

"I don't think we're supposed to do that."

"Why not?" she said.
"No one will know."

Then she pulled me into
another theater
to watch
another movie.
And then we went to her house,
where she showed me
the book of drawings she keeps.
Fairies,
elves,
dragons,
and wizards.

She is *such* a talented artist.

"When I turn eighteen," she told me,
"I'm going to get a bunch of these
as tatoos."

Yeah,
I don't think Jessa
needs to worry
anymore
about being
forgotten.

Jessa is definitely
unforgettable.

In the very best way,
of course.

The Truth Hurts

"Wanna shower? Go somewhere?" Zoe asks.

"We could cruise around in my new car," Jessa says.

"You got a new car?" I ask.
"What'd you get?"

"Well, it's used, but new to me.
It's a Mazda Protégé."

Wow.
Guess things are happening
out there
in the big, blue world.

"Come on," Cali says.
"Let's split this joint."

"Nah.
I'm not really up for anything today."

Jessa stands up.
"Ava, this isn't healthy.
It's beautiful out. Come on.
You're not the dead one, you know."

"Jessa!" Zoe yells.

"Oh, God," Cali says.
"Nice, Jessa."

"Sorry," Jessa says.
"I'm so sorry.
Forgive me?"

"You guys just don't have a clue what I'm going through," I say
as I pick at a loose thread on my robe.

"So tell us," Jessa says.
"We're here. Help us understand."

I stand up.

"I have stuff to do," I tell them,
which is a total lie
and they know it.
"Thanks for stopping by."

I walk to the door, open it, and wait.

"Bye, Ava."
"Bye, Hon."
"I'm sorry, A."

"Yeah," I tell them, in almost a whisper.
"It's okay.
See ya later."

I go to the front window
and watch their beautiful, tan bodies
get into Jessa's cute car.

They wave
and then the car
zips out of the driveway
and down the street
in a flash of silver.

The room gets cold.
Jackson is there.

"How come you can't go out, Jackson?
Do you *want* me here with you all the time?
I feel like you do.
Will you get mad at me if I go with my friends?
I mean, I have a *life*, Jackson.
Or, I should anyway.
Do you get that?"

No answer.

"Why can't ghosts TALK!?" I scream.

The Closest Thing to Talking

I sit on the couch
and cry
because everything is so
confusing
and mixed up.

Suddenly,
the music stops.

Oh, no.
No, please,
don't go!

I shouldn't have
screamed
like that.
This isn't his fault.
Does he hate me now?

I stand up
and call his name.
"Jackson?
JACKSON!?"

"Please come back," I shriek,
crying and pacing.
"Please don't leave me
by myself!"

When I feel the cold air
flutter around me
like a butterfly's wings,
I know he's back,
and I collapse on the
couch in relief.

"I'm sorry for yelling, Jackson.
I didn't mean it."

There's a whisper
inside my head
so soft,
I almost don't hear the first words.

There are ghost rules, Ava.
I'm not allowed to answer your questions.
I don't want to keep you from your friends.
I'm sorry I got mad before.
More than anything,
I want you to be happy.
I love you, Ava.
Be happy.

Road Trip

A few days before
the Fourth of July holiday,
they don't ask me,
they just do it.

Mom and Dad
whisk me away
to the place of
sand and sea,
with the never-ending sound
of waves
thrashing,
lashing,
crashing.

I love that sound.
I love the beach.

I've packed my windbreaker,
my sun visor,
my flip-flops
and tank tops.

What I couldn't pack
was my ghost of a boyfriend,
Jackson.

We're about to leave
when I say,
"Wait! I forgot something!"

I grab my key
from my purse,
run inside the house
and up the stairs.

"I'll miss you, Jackson," I say
to the still, quiet air
around me
as I walk toward
the bookcase in my room.
"I'll be back soon.
I promise."

I return to the car
with a stuffed
yellow snake
stuck in the pocket
of my hoody.

Let's Dance

I walk barefoot next to my mom.

The seagulls dance
across the sand
as the waves crash
on the shore.

The seagull waltz.

I dance around my mother's
topic of conversation.

"You don't talk about him.
Are you sure you're doing okay?"

"Yes."

"Ava, I'll just say it.
I'm worried about you.
It seemed like you were doing fine.
But lately, I don't know."

"I *am* fine, Mom."

She grabs my hand.
Squeezes it.
"I think it might be good for you to talk to someone."

"A shrink?"

"A grief counselor."

I stop walking
and let my eyes rest
on the blueness of the ocean,
thinking of Jackson,
wondering if he's sipping my lemonade
or drinking my cocoa
or frolicking around
in my panty drawer.

"Isn't it just so amazing, Mom?"

I put my arm around her
and put my head
on her shoulder.

"Sometimes, I think I smell him," she whispers.

I don't say anything.

The mother-daughter waltz.

Ghostly Tales

It's hard
to fall asleep
in a room
that isn't mine.

In the kite room
of the beach house,
kites are on every wall.
Blue ones,
red ones,
yellow ones,
and even one
shaped like a bird.

I quietly get up
and move over
to the computer.

I turn it on.
I Google "ghosts."

I click and read
click and read
click and read.

A website claiming to be
"The Number One Resource on Ghosts"
says that if a person dies with "unresolved issues"
or "emotional baggage,"
he can't move on
to "the higher plane."

Does Jackson have unresolved issues?
Or emotional baggage?
Do I want to know if he does?

I find a message board
on another site
where people share their experiences
and ask questions.

It seems like each ghost is different.
Some only appear once a year.
Some only appear in dreams.
Some only haunt houses.
Some only show up in mirrors.

Jackson seems to be
a do-anything
kind of ghost.

That makes sense
because he was pretty much
a do-anything
kind of guy.

Lost

The walls are thin.
My parents are talking.
Talking about *me*.

I tiptoe back to my bed.

Dad says, "The three girls and Nick
have been checking in with her, right?"

"Yes. But she still just sits at home most of the time."

"She needs to talk to someone."

"How do we get her to see she does?" Mom asks

"She doesn't have to see it.
She just has to do it.
We have to make her do it."

Oh. My. God.
My parents.
My friends.
They all
must think
I'm mental.

And Nick,
was he hitting on me
only because
he felt sorry for me?

I turn over
and cry into my pillow.

Jackson,
why aren't you here?
I need you!
If I sleep,
will you visit me?
Can you find me?

Please.
Find me.

Flying Alone

The kites
lift me up
and take me away
to a place where I sleep.

I sleep without dreams.
Without Jackson.

Finally,
I rest.

Good Morning

Sunday morning
I wake up early
for the first time
in a long time,
feeling refreshed.

I head to the beach, where
I want to run barefoot
on the sand,
feel the sea breeze
on my skin,
hear the ocean sounds
in my head.

Maybe it will help
me forget
all the mixed-up stuff
going on
in my life.

But I'm not the only one
who is up early.

A black Lab
runs over to me.
I bend down to pet him.
He drops a stick
at my feet.

"Sorry.
He loves to play fetch,"
says the tan guy
with short, blonde hair.

I laugh and say, "Okay."

Then I throw the stick into the ocean
and watch the dog
chase the stick
with everything
he's got.

Like if he loses that stick,
his life will never be the same.

The waves cover him
for a second,
but he bobs to the top
with the stick in his mouth.
And soon he is at my feet,
ready to play again.

"Good boy," I tell him.

His owner moves closer to me and says,
"His name is Bo."

"Good Bo." We laugh.

"And I'm Lyric."

"Lyric?
That's a cool name.
Do you sing?"

He breaks out
into an opera-style
rendition of
You Are My Sunshine.

I laugh and applaud.
He takes a bow.

"Wow.
So you're not shy," I tell him.

"Not shy at all," he says
as he sits
on a piece of driftwood
and pulls on my arm
so I'm sitting
right next to him.

Silly Nothingness

We people-watch
and talk
and laugh
about silly things,
like the Dallas Cowboys cheerleaders
(he likes football)
and how he thinks that's the easiest job in the world
and how I think, no way can that be even close to easy!

I wonder if he knows
I'm not capable
of anything more
than this.

I wonder
if he would care?

In the Moment

I am
talking,
and laughing,
and listening,
and talking some more.

Lyric is totally flirting with me,
which feels so weird
but flattering,
I guess.

He tells me a story
about a crazy friend of his
who's trying to beat
the pogo stick
world record,
and the way he talks about
bounce
bounce
bouncing
on that pogo stick
makes me laugh
hysterically.

And for the first time
in a long,
long
time,

I feel

A L I V E!

So Long, Farewell

Then I remember.
I remember him.
The one I will love forever
and the one who loves me so much
he can't leave me behind.

"I have to go," I say.

"Can I get your number?" he asks.

"I can't.
It's complicated."

I turn and walk away.
I don't want to say good-bye.
So I won't say anything.

Bo barks.
He says it for all of us.

"Drop me an e-mail," he calls out.
"It's Lyric@remstat.com."

I know he wants me to turn around
to say "okay"
or give a thumbs-up.
Something.
Anything.
I should turn and say,
I have a boyfriend.
I belong with him.
But the words refuse to come.

"I'll see you in my dreams, Ava," he calls to me.

I stop.
I get goose bumps.
I turn to make sure it's really Lyric,
and not
Jackson.

He waves,
and I wonder who I'll see
in my dreams
tonight.

Independence Day

I watch
the festivities
from the window.

Kids running,
waving sparklers.

Dads lighting
firecrackers.

Moms pulling kids back,
saying, "Don't stand too close."

The sky
fills with
red,
white,
and blue.

Into the darkness comes
light,
joy,
and freedom.

Tomorrow I go home
to Jackson.

I consider
what freedom
really means.

And I realize
maybe I'm not so free
after all.

It Doesn't Make Sense

As the car moves
toward home,
my thoughts
don't seem
to want to go there
just yet.

I didn't
want
to leave
the place of
salty air
and kite rooms
and lyrical boys.

Not only
did I survive
the days
which I didn't think
I could,
they refreshed me,
revitalized me,
reminded me
of what I've been
missing.

What does that mean
exactly?

My thoughts
don't seem
to want to go *there*
just yet
either.

Back Home

It's late
when we get home.
I feel my pulse
quicken
as I think
about Jackson,
hoping he won't be too upset.

The house is quiet.
Dark.
Normal.

Mom and Dad go to bed.
I make a PB&J sandwich.

I wait for movement
or music
or mind messages.

But there's nothing.

I eat,
then go to my room.

My room is quiet.
Dark.
Normal.

I go to the bathroom, where
I stand at the mirror
long after I'm done
brushing and washing.

Finally, I go to bed,
wondering if he'll find me
in my dreams,
and sort of praying
he won't.

Light the Way

I wake up
in the middle of the night
to candles
lit up
in the darkness.

"Jackson," I whisper,
"that's sweet,
but you can't do things like that.
What if my mom or dad walks in?"

A gust of wind
blows across the room
and in an instant
the room
turns
black.

Sorry.

"No, Jackson.
I'm sorry.
I'm sorry this is so hard."

And I wonder when I'll finally
stop having things
to feel sorry about.

What's Going On?

No one called
while we were away.

No one calls
after we return.

I spend time
watching TV,
playing solitaire
on the computer,
and reading magazines.

Jackson hangs around
some of the time.

But I still wish
someone
would
pick up the
phone
and
talk
to
me.

To Go or Not to Go

Days go by
and I finally
call Cali.

Why have I been
such a bad friend?

What happened to the good friend
who'd pick a bouquet of daisies for Cali
or make peanut butter cookies for Jessa
or burn a CD of songs for Zoe?

I miss flowers
and cookies
and music.

I want to feel
like a friend again.

"What's up?" I ask.

"Uh, I'm getting ready to head out," she says.

"Gotta hot date?"

"Sort of."

"Really?
With who?"

"A bunch of people are going to—"

She stops.
I wait.
She doesn't finish.

"Oh no," I say.
"Not there."

"Ava, it's time.
It's not an evil place, you know.
Kids are hanging out there as a tribute to him.
It's like you can feel his spirit there.
Really.
There's even been talk of changing the name.
You know, to Jackson's Hideaway."

"But Cali, he died there.
How can people have fun at the place where he *died*?"

"I'm going," she says.
"You could come too.
It might be good for you, actually."

"Cali, I called because I need to talk to you.
Please?
Can we go have a mocha?
And I'll think about going.
I will."

Well,
Cali never could
turn down a mocha.

No Secrets

We sip on our mochas
at Starbucks,
where we've
spent hours upon hours
talking
and giggling
like girls do.

My heart tells me
it's time to spill my guts.

After all,
I used to tell her
everything.

I told her about the time
I snuck out one night
to meet Jackson
down the corner
so we could make out
on the back porch
of the vacant house.

I even told her about the time
I kissed Nick
at midnight
on New Year's Eve
when I was still going with Jackson
but he was out of town
and I was lonely.

And now I tell her about how
Jackson is in my house
and how he turns the CD player on
and how he appears in mirrors
and how he sends me messages
in his own little ways
and visits me in my dreams.

"Are you saying he's a ghost?" she asks.

"Basically. Yeah."

And then she gives me
the look.
That look
that says,
"Girlfriend,
you have totally
gone off the
d
e
e
p

e
n
d."

Stop It!

She rolls up
the corner of her napkin.

She fiddles with the
packets of sugar.

She looks around,
like she wants to escape,
but doesn't know how.

"I'm not crazy," I say.

"He's gone, A.
I know you miss him.
But you've got to move on."

"Maybe you should come and see for yourself."

"So, you see him?" she asks.

"No. Well, yes, in my dreams I do.
But in the house, he's just there.
I feel him.
I smell him.
He lets me know he's there. In little ways.
Even Mom says she's smelled him.
Sandalwood shaving cream, you know."

"So your mom thinks he's a ghost, too?" she asks.

"No. She just mentioned that she thought she smelled him.
An observation.
But don't you see, it's because he *is* there."

She shakes her head,
stands up,
and grabs her purse.

"You want to go with me or should I take you home?"

I don't know
what I want to do.
It scares me to think about
going there again.

I look at Cali.
That look is still
on her face.

I'm *not* crazy!

Maybe
there's only one way
to prove it.

"Okay. I'll go."

Absolutely Perfect

We named it
Heaven's Hideaway.

Who knew
that name
would take on
a whole new
meaning.

Hidden back
behind the
towering green trees
is a place
right out of
a fairy tale
with a cascading waterfall
and a large, deep pool of water
surrounded by
rocks
and grass
and ferns
and plants
and flowers.

I told Jackson,
"This must be
what heaven looks like."

And so, it had a name.

I'm the One

Jackson and Daniel
discovered it one day
on a hike.

He couldn't wait
to show me
the special place.

We packed a lunch
and it wasn't long before
I found myself
having the most
perfect picnic
ever.

I loved the place
so much.

I'm the one
who came up with the idea.

I'm the one
who said it'd be the perfect place
for the School's Out party.

I'm the one
who's wished
a million times over
I never
ever
did.

What a Surprise

Cali and I arrive,
and the party's
going strong.

Someone's set a
boom box
on a rock,
and the heavy thumps drown out
the peacefulness
of the place.
The peacefulness
that Jackson and I found
the first time we came here
together.

I want to focus
on that time,
not the other time, the last time,
but it's too hard
to keep the memories
from cascading
into my brain.

I shouldn't have come.
It's too soon.

Way
too
soon.

"Cali—"

But I don't get a chance to finish.
A chance to tell her
I shouldn't be here.

"Oh, there he is," Cali says,
grabbing my arm.
Squeezing it.

He?
Who's he???

And then she's off
to greet him.
I watch
and wait,
to see who
he
is.

Lyric!?

A Rush of Emotions

Cali wraps her arms
around Lyric's neck and
hugs him.

They do not kiss.

So, that means
a) they haven't known each other long
or
b) they're just friends
or
c) she likes him, but he doesn't necessarily like her.

She pulls on his arm
and they walk toward me.

"Ava, do you know Lyric?
He was a senior last year.
Running back on the football team.
Number 11."

Lyric? At our school?
How come I never noticed him before?

Ummm, yeah,
probably because
he was a senior
and way out of my league
and I had a boyfriend
who made me
deliriously
happy.

"Hi."

"Hi."

He smiles that beach boy smile of his,
and right then I discover
a person has the ability
to feel
a hundred different emotions
all at the same time.

Feeling Woozy

I look at Lyric
and hope he knows
he shouldn't say
anything
about me and him.

"I need to sit down," I tell Cali.
"Catch my breath."

"Are you okay?" she asks.

"I'm fine.
Just a lot, you know, to take in."

"You're white as a ghost," Lyric says.

How appropriate.

"Want me to sit with you?" she asks.

"No. Go! Have fun.
I'll come find you guys in a minute."

They head for the crowd
while I head away from it.
I don't want to talk to anyone.
And I'm pretty sure
no one really
wants to talk to me.

What do you say
to the girl
who was the dead boy's
girlfriend?

What do you say
to the girl
who is looking at the place
where it happened?

What do you say
to the girl
who dared her boyfriend
to jump
that deadly day?

All. My. Fault.

I traveled to Hawaii
with my parents
when I was twelve.

We went to this place
where people dove
off the cliffs
into the
cool
blue
waters
below.

For some
totally random reason,
on that partying
day in May,
I thought of those
adrenaline junkies
who were so much
like Jackson.

Then I said those
three
stupid
words
and Jackson's eyes
moved toward the sky,
like a vulture eying his prey,

as he considered
the greatest
challenge
yet.

He climbed up high.
Way high.
He spread out his arms,
like Jesus on the cross,
and shouted,
"This is going to be so great!"

Suddenly
I knew.
I knew it was a
bad
idea.

I screamed, "STOP!"

just a
second
too
late.

When Two Became One

We waited
for him to
pop up
laughing,
SHOUTING,
b r e a t h i n g.

We didn't hear
his head
hit the rock.

We didn't hear
his cries
of pain.

We didn't hear
his last breath.

Deadly
silence
floated
on the water
like an empty raft.

Rescue instincts
kicked in and
I rushed to the water,
hit it hard,
and began to
stroke
stroke
stroke

like my life depended on it,
because my life *SO* depended on it.

As I swam,
brain-photos
appeared.

Whirling,
swirling,
twirling
images
of football games,
of starry nights,
of carnival rides.

I wasn't the
only one
in the water.

A mob
of people
took hold of him
and then I
was
whirling,
swirling,
twirling
in the sea of red
left behind.

The water,
my friend forever,
enveloped me,

whispering,
Stay here.
Let me take care of you.
Rest in my comforting arms.

It knew.

But other arms
grabbed me
and pulled me
from heaven
into hell.

I lay on the ground,
frozen from fear.
Trees towered above me,
shaking their wooden fingers at me.

Screams
of hysteria
flew through the air,
slamming into
each other.

"Call 911 . . . He's not breathing . . . Oh my God, oh my God . . .
Do something . . ."

Three big words
drowned them all out.

I killed Jackson.

I Need Dorothy's Shoes

The memories
literally
make
me
sick.

As I hug the tree
and lose my mocha,
all I can think about
is how I want to go home.
I need to go home.

Only problem is,
I left my cell at home,
so I can't call my mom
to come and get me.

I gather myself
and my thoughts
and look for Cali.

I find her in the middle
of a group of kids
grooving it,
shaking it,
moving it.

"Cali," I shout, "I need your phone."

"How come?"

"Just because."

"It's in my purse.
Over there," she says
as she waves her hand
in a big, generic swoop
in no particular direction.

I turn around
and run
right into Nick,
who's holding hands
with a pretty little thing.

"Hey, Ava!
So great to see you!"

He gives me a quick hug,
then turns to the girl.

"This is Krystal."

"Hi there," I blurt out.
"Nick, can I use your phone?"

"Sorry, it's in my car."

"Crap."

My head is spinning,
my stomach is churning,
my heart is aching,
and I don't know
what to do.

And then, Lyric's there,
pulling me away.
Away from
the music,
the laughing,
the noisy noise,
and into the quiet
of the forest.

"I have a phone you can use," he tells me.
"Who do you want to call?"

"My mom.
I need a ride.
I shouldn't have come."

And before I even know what's happening,
I'm in his sweet red jeep,
heading home.

Tears of What?

You'd think
riding in a jeep,
feeling the wind across my face,
and listening to Black Eyed Peas jam it out
with a cute guy by my side
would make me
happy.

No.

It makes me cry.
Or maybe I'm crying
for other reasons.
It's hard to tell
when there are a hundred emotions,
all mixed up together.

He reaches over
and holds my hand
and something about that
calms me down
and the tears
stop flowing.

When we get to town,
he pulls into
the parking lot
of Taco Del Mar.

"I thought maybe we'd get a bite to eat
before I take you home.

I want to make sure you're okay."

I nod. "Sure."

And so we go inside.
He orders.
I sit.

When he sits down
across from me,
he says, "I'm sorry I didn't put it together
at the beach that you were *that* Ava."

"Sorry?"

"I just mean, you're going through a lot.
And I should have been, you know,
more sensitive, or whatever."

"Are you always so *nice*?" I ask.

He smiles.

And when I get goose bumps
all over my body
because of that smile
and I think about what
a terrible girlfriend I am to Jackson,
I start to cry
all over again.

My Nose Rejoices

It's hard to cry
in a restaurant
with napkins
as tissues
and people staring.

But Lyric
comes over to sit beside me,
puts his arm around me,
and lets me bury my face
into his soft
baby blue t-shirt
that smells like
soap
and deodorant
and real,
live
boy.

A Real, Live Boy _Friend_

When I finally pull away,
he looks down at me and says,
"You were pretty brave to go back there.
Do you want to talk about it?"

I shake my head.
"I think we need to change the subject or something.
Unless you like your shirt _really_ damp."

He laughs. "Okay.
We'll talk about something else.
Let me get you something to drink."

He comes back
with the order and some drinks,
and sits across from me again.
No more touching
the real
live
boy.

"So, I'm curious about Cali," I say.
"Where did you two meet?"

"The bookstore.
Where I work.
Just a couple of weeks ago, actually."

"Are you going out?"

"Nah.

I don't really know her.
There's this other girl I like.
But she won't give me her number.
So, I guess we'll just be friends."

It makes me smile.

He smiles back,
and it feels like
we've been friends
forever.

A friend is good.

A girl can *never*
have too many friends.

So Long, Again

He drives me home.
We say good-bye.
Nothing else really.

I don't have to tell him.
He seems to understand
it's just too soon.

It is.

And what I know
is this:
I have
Jackson.

But is Jackson
who I really
want?

Thinking Too Hard

I shouldn't even be thinking that question,
but it keeps popping up.

It's there
like a dull headache
that won't go away.

I sit on the couch
and turn the TV on
and think about
my dilemma.

I still love him.
I will always love him.
But him is the Jackson I knew.
The walking,
talking,
breathing
Jackson.

I'm just not sure
I can wholly
and completely
with everything I am
be satisfied
loving
a ghost.

And then I feel the coldness.

"Jackson," I whisper.
"You're here."

Can he hear my thoughts?
Does he know?

An image of Lyric
darts in.
I shake my head.
It doesn't help.

What is *wrong* with me????

Forever in Debt

The thing is,
I owe it to Jackson
to be here
for him.

I owe him that much.

If it weren't for *me*,
he wouldn't even be a ghost.

Whatever he wants,
I have to give him.

It sounds *so* easy.

It should
be
easy!

But repaying a debt
means giving up things.
Making sacrifices.

If I sacrifice my heart
for Jackson,
will I be dead
too?

Normal Is Nice

Jackson sits with me.
He plays with the TV
from time to time,
making the channels turn.

At first it makes me smile.
Then it gets on my nerves.

Big time.

Because he can't talk
like a normal guy.
He can't hold hands
like a normal guy.
He can't kiss
like a normal guy.
Unless it's in my dreams,
and then we do those last two things.
But dreaming about them
isn't the same
as actually
doing them
and *experiencing* them.

All he can really *do*
are the strange ghostly things
that let me know
he's here.

Don't worry, Jackson.
I know you're here.

Believe me.
I know.

He flicks the gas fireplace on
even though it's like ninety degrees outside.

"Jackson," I yell,
"stop being so *weird*."

And then
it hits me like
a fast,
open-palmed,
stinging
SMACK
in the face.

Having a ghost
for a boyfriend
is
weird.

I Want to Know How

The phone rings
as Mom walks in the door
carrying pizza
for dinner.

"Are you okay?" asks Nick
when I pick up the phone.

For some reason,
it makes me laugh.

"Is that the only sentence you know?"

He doesn't laugh.

"It just seemed like you were upset.
When I saw you earlier."

"Yeah. I was.
But I'm okay.
Thanks, Nick.
I guess you're not so bad after all.
And Krystal's really cute."

"She's great.
You'd like her."

He pauses for a second.

"You know, I didn't want to let you go," he says.
"I liked you a lot, and I'm sorry I hurt you.

I held on, hoping things might change.
Then New Year's Eve gave me more hope.
I held on, longer than I should have."

"So now you've let go?"

"Well, I still care about you.
But yeah, I think I finally have."

"Was it hard?" I ask.
"Letting go?"

"Not as hard as holding on to something that wasn't real."

I gulp. "Can I ask how you did it?"

"I just decided, Ava.
That's all.
I just decided."

No Rest for the Weary

This time,
I stay awake.

I avoid sleep
like my life
depends on it.

And maybe,
life,
true life,
does depend on it.

If Jackson comes into a room,
I leave
and go
someplace else.

He follows me
more than he ever has before.
Maybe he senses
the uncertainty
that has crept
into my heart.

As always,
he leaves me alone
when Mom or Dad
are there.

At night,
I curl up
in the corner of their bedroom
and listen to
Dad's faint snoring noises
and Mom's soft breathing sounds
and wish
I could sleep
peacefully
like that.

But I've got to stay awake.
I've got to keep distance
between Jackson

and me.

Thanks, Mom

On Sunday,
I curl up
with Mom
on the couch
and we watch
Steel Magnolias
on TNT.

When I was younger,
I always
spent Sundays
with Mom.

She'd paint my toenails.
Braid my hair.
Rub my back.

Nothing extreme.
But *so* completely satisfying.

"This gets sad," she says.

"I know. It's okay."

"You look tired."

You'd look tired too
if you hadn't slept a minute
in two whole days.

I lay down
with my head in her lap
and she strokes my hair.

"I wish I could make it better," she whispers.

And as I drift to sleep, I think,
You are, Mom.
You are.

A Million Apologies

He is there,
in my dream,
but I don't let him
touch me.
Not this time.

This time,
he has to let me say it.

"Jackson, do you know how sorry I am?
Do you know if I could change places with you, I would?"

He comes closer.
I step back.

"You have to listen to me," I tell him.
"You have to understand.
It's my fault,
and I'm *so* sorry.
So terribly sorry!
sorrysorrysorrysorrysorrysorry
sorrysorrysorrysorrysorrysorry

"Jackson, please forgive me.
Please!"

"It's okay, Ava.
Ava?
AVA!?!?"

A Real-Life Nightmare

Mom is shaking me
and yelling my name
to wake me up.

"Ava, are you all right?
You were thrashing around and crying out
like someone was hurting you."

"Mom, it hurts *so* much.
All of it.
I just want it to go away."

I want to tell her *so* bad.
I want to tell her everything.
Except she won't believe me.
Just like Cali didn't believe me.

And if Mom and Dad
don't believe me,
they'll think I'm Crazy Girl
and send me away.

I sit up
and burst into tears
while I dissolve
into her arms.

"Shhhhhh," she says
over
and over
again.

And then I know
there is something
I have to tell her.

I pull myself away and
look at her.

"It was my fault, Mom.
I dared him. What was I thinking? I wasn't thinking.
Don't you see?
He did it for *me*."

Hard to Believe

I want to believe her
when she tells me
it wasn't my fault
and that I have to stop
blaming myself.

She says, "It wasn't you, Ava.
He made the choice.
Do you understand?
You did *not* push him off that ledge."

I want to believe her
with every bone in my body.

But that is pretty much impossible
when every bone in my body
feels
so
incredibly
guilty.

One Boy and Two Girls

Cali calls Sunday night.

"Jessa said you left the party with Lyric."

"Yeah, he took me home.
I wasn't feeling too well.
I shouldn't have went with you."

"That was nice of him to do that," she says,
and I wonder if I hear
a hint of jealousy in her voice.

She goes on.
"I keep hoping he'll call me.
You know, to ask me out.
Did he say anything about me?"

"Just that you met at the bookstore.
Where he works."

"I think I'll go by tomorrow and see him."
She pauses. "Wanna go with me?"

I want to say yes.
But not because of her.
Because of him.
And there's something
horribly
wrong in that.

"I really like him," she says.

"I know," I say.
"You should go and see him by yourself."

Because I really like him too.

Friends

After we hang up,
I turn the computer on.

I have an e-mail from Nick.

Says it was good to talk to me
and we should do it more often.
Says I've got to meet Krystal.
We should get together.
Says he is glad we are friends.

I have an e-mail from Jessa.

Says she's sorry
she didn't get to talk to me
at the party.
Says it was good to see me
out in the world.
Says she loves me
with lots of xo's.

I write her a note that tells her
we'll get together soon
and I miss her.

Then I start a new message.

TO: Lyric@remstat.com

my phone number is: 222-1567
ttyl
ava

And then, before I have any time
to change my mind,
I hit
SEND.

Mother Knows Best

I stay awake
again
Sunday night.

Monday morning, Dad leaves early.
He's heading to Montreal
for the week.

Mom has work to do
and I think about asking her
to stay home with me.
But then she'd
really
worry.

She reaches out
and cups the back of my head
in her hand
in a way that says
I love you.

"Will you do something fun today?
Call one of the girls.
Go to the mall. Or the pool.
Something?"

"Maybe."

Her eyes search mine.
What is she looking for?
The old Ava?
The happy Ava?
The Ava who didn't carry guilt around
like a big boulder on her shoulders?

"Sweetheart," she says,
almost in a whisper,
"I'm making an appointment for you.
To talk to someone.
I know you don't want to.
But I think you need to."

I can tell,
by her face,
her voice,
her touch,
she's made up her mind.

So I nod
and secretly wonder
what else I might need to do
that I don't really want
to do.

Get Me Out of Here

Then I'm back to today
and what I should do
with the day
that looms ahead of me
like a long,
lonely
road.

"I wish I could drive," I tell Mom.

"It's not long till your sweet sixteen," she says.

"I'm not so sure it will be very sweet."

She kisses my cheek and says,
"It will be because you are."
And then she leaves.

Once again
I'm left
with just my thoughts
and the ghost
who haunts me
because
he loves me.

I need to do
something.

If I stay here,
I'm not sure

I can stay awake
any longer.

The cool air comes.
I shiver.
The music turns on.

 My Last Breath
by Evanescence.

I don't want to
hear these words.

It's a sad song.
Does he want me to feel sad?
If I feel sad,
does he think that will
make my heart
want him more?

He is closer to me now.
So close.
I think I feel
his breath
on my cheek.

And then the phone rings.

It startles me.
I run to answer it.

"Hello?"

"Ava?"

It's the lyrical voice
of the real, live boy.

"Were you sleeping?"

"No. I'm awake."

I don't tell him
I'm avoiding sleep
to avoid
my ghost of a boyfriend.

"I don't have to work today.
Wanna go have lunch? See a movie?"

But there's Cali.
And there's Jackson.
And there's—
me.

"Pick me up this afternoon?
Around one?"

Who Are You?

The music gets loud.
And louder still.

He might be mad.
Does he know
it was a boy
on the phone?

Or is he just tired
of me ignoring him?

I feel him near me
as I go into the bathroom.
I shut the door
and lock it behind me,
but it doesn't
keep him out.

"Jackson,
can I have a little privacy?
Please?"

He doesn't leave.
I feel him there,
so close.
If he were alive,
our skin
would be touching,
chest to chest,
legs entwined,
arms wrapped
around each other.

But he's not alive.
As much as I might wish
and as much as he might wish,
he's
not
alive.

This time I yell.
"Jackson, leave me alone!"

The water in the sink
turns on
full blast.

I go to turn it off,
and as I do,
I glance in the mirror
and his face
appears,
just for a second.

It's not the face
of the beautiful,
joyful,
loving
boy
I used to know.

It is a dark,
sullen,
painfully sad face
that scares me so bad
I want to turn and
run and
never ever
come back.

I Have to Say It

And so I run.

I run from the bathroom
and back to the kitchen.

The hauntingly familiar music
of Evanescence still plays.

I go to the CD player
and change the song
to track 4.
My Immortal.

It speaks of a girl
being tied to a life she doesn't want
and how she's haunted in her dreams.

I let the music fill the room,
and then I yell with everything inside of me,

"Jackson, you have to go.
This isn't working.
Don't you see?
This isn't what love is supposed to be like."

I crumble
into a chair
in the kitchen.

I love
you
and
I'm sorry,
he barely whispers
in my mind.

The fatigue,
the sadness,
the fear,
the *guilt*
all come to the surface,
and then I'm crying,
shaking,
pulling at my hair,
shrieking in a voice
that doesn't sound like mine.

"YOU
HAVE
TO GO!

"I CAN'T
LIVE
LIKE
THIS!"

It Hurts to Breathe

I think I'm starting
to hyperventilate.
I run and grab a bag
out of the drawer.

In
Out
In
Out

I breathe slowly
and try to
calm down
so I can finish
what I need to say.

I hurt everywhere.
I ache with the pain
I feel
because I have to
do this.

"I'm sorry, Jackson.
I will always love you.
I will always remember what we had.

"But you have to move on.
You don't belong here.

"I wish I could change everything and erase that day.
But I can't.

"You have to go.
Please, Jackson.
Please go."

On One Condition

Okay.
I will go.
But only if
you will give me
your guilt
to take
with me.

But How?

So *that*
is his unresolved
issue.

He doesn't want
to leave me behind,
carrying around
a blanket of blame.

I put my head
in my hands
and weep
for the loss of
Jackson.

My soul
cries
like it has
never
cried before.

He is
so
good.

His love
for me is
so true.

I remember
the notes
he left me.

Ava is good . . .
Be happy . . .
Don't be blue . . .

It wasn't
about him.

It was
about
me
and wanting me
to live
the rest of my life
with joy,
instead of
grief
and pain.

He doesn't blame me.
But I blame myself.

How do I rid my heart
of that guilt
and let
go?

Maybe
Nick
had the answer.

Maybe
I just
decide.

Maybe
right now,
in this moment,
I decide
that it's sad
and tragic
and painful,
but feeling bad
and blaming myself
won't
bring
him back.

And maybe
there is one more thing
I can do.

Letting Go

I sit down at the computer.
I open Word and start typing.

The words come freely,
easily, as if
my hands
have been waiting for the opportunity
to speak.

Dear Mom and Dad:

You know those nights, when you look up, and it's so clear
you feel like you can see every single star in the universe?
And there's always one star that shines the brightest. The star
we focus on when we say, "Star light, star bright . . ."

Jackson was that star in my world. He made my world brighter.
I miss him so much.

When I look out at the stars now, I wish with everything I have
that Jackson was still here. Every day, I've wished.

But today, I'm wondering something. What is Jackson's wish for me?

I think his wish for me is this:

Joy, not sorrow.

Laughter, not tears.

Life, not death.

Love, not blame.

I want to make his wishes come true.

Thank you for being the best parents a girl could ever have.

Love,
Ava

I could leave it on the counter,
but something tells me
to make it official.

So I seal it in an envelope,
address it,
and find a stamp in the desk.

And then I walk outside
into the warm and inviting sunshine
and mail my letter.

I See You

I turn to head inside
and I see him.

I stop.
My feet won't move.

He is floating
behind the window.

He looks different
than before.

More at peace.
Not so sad.
More like
the Jackson
I used to know.

That's my girl.
Live a good life, Ava.

And then,
he disappears
and I'm left looking at
my own reflection
in the glass.

I look
more at peace.
Not so sad.
More like
the me
I used to know.

Good-bye Forever

When I come back inside,
the music has stopped.

The house
is peacefully
quiet.

I sit down
and the tears fall
softly this time.

I don't have to go looking,
searching the house,
standing by mirrors,
waiting.
My heart knows.
He's gone.

He loved me enough
to let me go.

Now I have to do
my part.

No guilt.
No regrets.
No shame.

I must
start living
again.

Good-bye, Jackson.
I will LOVE you 4ever.

Wake-up Call

I think I cry
myself to sleep.

I wake up
to the sound of the doorbell
ringing
over
and over
again.

I barely make it to the door.
It feels like I've taken
twenty pills
and can't wake up.

As I open the door,
I remember.

Lyric.

"You *were* sleeping," he says.

I smile. "Yeah."

I invite him in,
rubbing my eyes,
thinking how terrible
I must look.

"So, you still want to go?" he asks.

"Can you wait right here?
I'll be back."

He smiles and nods.

And then I run upstairs
to the bathroom
because my breath
has got to be
atrocious.

Matchmaker

I brush my teeth,
brush my hair,
brush a little blush on my cheeks,
and call it good.

It doesn't really matter.
I know that.
But it gives me the confidence
to do
what I realize
I have to do.

I go back down
and he has the remote in his hand,
flipping through
the channels.

I sit down.
He turns it off.

I smile.
He smiles.

"I'm guessing, by the look on your face,
you've changed your mind," he says.

This is one
insightful
dude.

"Lyric, you are such a great guy.
And you know, you and Cali would make a fantastic couple.
She loves tacos and dogs and football, just like you.
I want you to call her. Get to know her."

"But—," he starts.

"No.
Please.
Don't.

"My heart has lots of stuff it has to work through.
Throwing you into the mix, it just wouldn't be fair.
For me or for you."

He reaches over
and hugs me.

"Still friends, right?" I ask.

He smiles. "Yeah. Still friends."

I walk him outside,
and as he gets in his jeep,
I don't tell him
good-bye.

I yell out,
"Call Cali!"

I'm Definitely a Dog Person

Guilt reminds me
of a stray
cat.

You chase it away
and yet,
it comes back
when you least
expect it.

If you let yourself
feel pity for it and
feed the thing,
it parks its ugly,
puny,
lonely-for-attention
butt
on your doormat
and
won't
go
away.

Mom and Dad
watch me
write notes
to myself
and stick them
around the house.

Joy, Not Sorrow

Laughter, Not Tears

Life, Not Death

They smile at me.
They got the letter.
They understand.

Scat,
kitty cat,
scat.
I don't need you
sitting around here
like that.

The Perfect Gift

On my birthday,
my girlfriends
take me out
to a Mexican restaurant,
where we sip on virgin margaritas
while the waiters put a sombrero
on my head
and sing to me.

It's definitely
a *sweet* birthday
and I'm so blown away
by my friends
being there
and loving me
through everything.

Maybe Mom did ask them
to check in on me.
But maybe they would have anyway.
Maybe they weren't sure
what to say to me
or how to help me.
They tried,
and I love them
for that.

As I look at my gifts,
the bracelet Cali made for me,
the new books Zoe bought for me,
the framed drawing Jessa made for me,
I feel thankful
for the best gift of all.

It's the one wrapped around my heart
with a big, pink bow—

the never-ending gift
of friendship.

Another Good Friend

I return,
accompanied only by
my new driver's license,
for a visit
before summer
takes its final bow
and autumn
hits the stage.

The water glistens
as the rays
of the late afternoon sun
shine down
upon it.

It's more inviting
than a down comforter bed
on a cold, winter night.

I've stayed away
from my old friend
far too long.

I didn't visit at Zoe's party.
I didn't visit at the beach.
I didn't visit the last time I was here.

I've missed you, friend.
I don't blame you.
I never did.

Maybe I was scared.
Maybe it needed to mean something.
Maybe it just didn't feel right.

I tear off my tank top and shorts,
but before I jump in,
I look up.

I swear he is there,
his arms outstretched,
the waterfall beneath him,
cascading into the
cool
blue
water
below.

Go on, Ava. It's going to be great!

It's not a dare.
Not this time.
But it's almost like I'm on that high dive again,
scared of what comes next,
yet knowing at the same time
it will all be
okay.

The water's cold,
but I can feel
Jackson's smile
shining down on me,
as bright and warm
as the summer sunshine,
when he sees me wearing
the black-and-pink
bikini.

Ava

"Tell me about yourself," Dr. Andrews asked me,
during our first session.

I thought Dr. Andrews
would be a lady
with ugly glasses
and hair in a bun
and a clipboard
where she scribbled things
like
LUNATIC
CRAZY GIRL
GUILTY AS HELL.

Instead
she is pretty,
with curly red hair,
and there isn't any
clipboard.

When I visit her,
I sit in a comfy brown chair
and we talk.

I've realized therapy
is incredibly
therapeutic.

When she asked me
to talk about myself,
I wasn't sure what to say.

"You mean things I like?"

"I'd love to know what's special about Ava."

I thought,
I could tell her how I've always loved to swim,
how I love music, movies, and shopping,
how I loved having a boyfriend
who clicked with me
from the very first second,
and how my friends
mean everything to me.

Then I thought,
too bad I'm not as much fun as Cali
or as determined as Zoe
or as brave and confident as Jessa.

They're each *so* special.

"I don't know," I told her.
"There's nothing special, really."

"Was it special being Jackson's girlfriend?" she asked.

"Very."

She leaned forward in her chair,
like a flower in a vase,
reaching for a glimpse
of the sun.

"There are other things special about Ava Bender.
You just need to discover those things again.
Will you make a list?
And then you can share them with me when you're ready."

Now, as I drive along
the curvy roads
heading home from
Jackson's Hideaway,
I remember the list
I have so far.

I am warm-hearted.
I am affectionate.
I am reliable.
I am generous.
I am smart.
I am strong.

Today,
I add another one.

I am hopeful.

About the Author

ALTHOUGH LISA SCHROEDER HAS BEEN A FAN OF VERSE NOVELS for a long time, she'd never written one until she had a dream about Ava and Jackson. She was literally haunted by their story until she finally wrote it down.

Lisa, a native Oregonian, lives in a yellow house surrounded by lots of lovely flowers and plants (thanks to her husband, who has an entire green hand). She is mom to two fabulous sons and is the official dog walker in the family. Since the age of eight, Lisa has been writing books, and to prove it, she has one about a lion that her grandma stuck in a drawer and saved. If you peek into Lisa's house in the wee hours of the morning, you'll usually find her typing away at the keyboard with a cup of tea by her side. You can visit her at www.lisaschroederbooks.com.

AMANDA MARRONE   LISA McMANN

MOVE OUTSIDE THE REALM OF NORMAL

WITH THESE DANGEROUSLY GOOD BOOKS.

KRISTOPHER REISZ   LISA SCHROEDER

 FROM SIMON PULSE | PUBLISHED BY SIMON & SCHUSTER

What if you could see your best friend's dreams?
How about your crush's?
Or a stranger's?

YOUR DREAMS ARE NOT YOUR OWN

WAKE

LISA McMANN

She can't tell anybody about what she does—
they'd never believe her, or, worse,
they'd think she's a freak. . . .

From Simon Pulse
PUBLISHED BY SIMON & SCHUSTER

FIND YOUR EDGE WITH THESE STARTLING AND STRIKING BOOKS—ALL FROM FIRST-TIME NOVELISTS.

JASON MYERS **AMANDA MARRONE** **KRISTOPHER REISZ**

Gritty. Electrifying. Real.

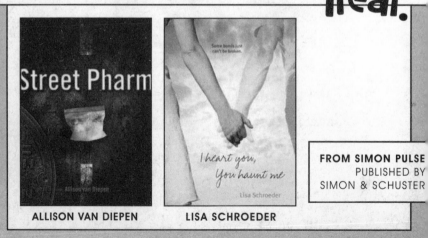

ALLISON VAN DIEPEN **LISA SCHROEDER**

FROM SIMON PULSE
PUBLISHED BY
SIMON & SCHUSTER

PULSE it

Did you **love** this book?

Want to get the
hottest books **free**?

Log on to
www.SimonSaysTEEN.com
to find out how you can get
free books from **Simon Pulse**
and become part of our **IT Board**,
where you can tell **US**, what **you** think!

SIMON
PULSE